.75

This book belongs to:

Rebecca Kazdan

D0949451

Published by Ladybird Books Ltd
27 Wrights Lane London W8 5TZ
A Penguin Company
3 5 7 9 10 8 6 4

TEXT © LADYBIRD BOOKS LTD MCMXCVIII
ILLUSTRATIONS © ROBERT MCPHILLIPS MCMXCVIII

Printed in Italy

The Wizard of Oz

illustrated by Robert McPhillips

Ladybird

Once upon a time, there was a little girl called Dorothy. Dorothy lived on a farm in Kansas, America. She lived with her aunt, her uncle and her little dog, Toto.

One day, Dorothy's aunt and uncle were out working on the farm. Dorothy was in the farmhouse playing with Toto.

Suddenly, a whirlwind came and carried the farmhouse away. Dorothy was very frightened.

"Where are we going to land?" she said to her little dog.

They came down in a land full of flowers.

Suddenly, a beautiful lady appeared.

"Where am I?" said Dorothy.

"You are in the land of Oz," said the lady. "I am very pleased to see you. I am the Good Witch." She thanked Dorothy for killing the Wicked Witch.

"What Wicked Witch?" said Dorothy.

"Look under your farmhouse," said the Good Witch.

Dorothy looked under the farmhouse. There she saw a witch. On the witch's feet were two magic shoes.

Dorothy put on the shoes.

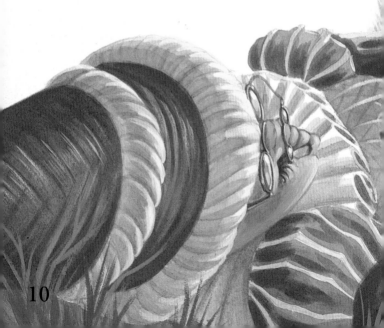

"I want to go back home," said Dorothy. "How do I get there?"

"You must go to see the Wizard of Oz," said the Good Witch. "He lives in the Emerald City, along the yellow brick road. He can help you."

"Can you come with me?" said Dorothy.

"No," said the Good Witch. "But I will be there when you need me."

So Dorothy and Toto followed the yellow brick road. Soon, they saw a scarecrow.

"Where are you going?" asked the scarecrow.

"We're going to the Emerald City, to see the Wizard of Oz," said Dorothy.

"I'll come with you," said the scarecrow. "My head is full of straw. I want to ask the Wizard for some brains, so that I can think."

So Dorothy, Toto and the scarecrow followed the yellow brick road.

They passed a man made of tin.

"Are you going to see the Wizard of Oz?" asked the tin man.

"Yes," said Dorothy.

"Can I come with you?" said the tin man. "I want to ask the Wizard for a heart, so that I can love."

So they all walked along the yellow brick road.

Suddenly, an angry lion appeared.

"Where are you all going?"
asked the lion.

"We're going to the Emerald City
to see the Wizard of Oz,"
said Dorothy.

21

"Can I come, too?" said the lion. "I want to ask him for some courage. It's no good being a lion without courage."

Dorothy was happy with her new friends. They all followed the yellow brick road together.

Soon, Dorothy, Toto, the scarecrow, the tin man and the lion came to the Emerald City. Everything in the city was made of emeralds. A little man appeared.

"We want to see the Wizard of Oz," said Dorothy. "Can you take us to him?"

"Follow me," said the little man. And he took them to a beautiful emerald room.

There they saw the Wizard of Oz.

Dorothy and her friends were frightened.

"Wizard, can you help us?" asked Dorothy.

"What do you want me to do?" said the Wizard.

"I'd like a brain," said the scarecrow.

"I'd like a heart," said the tin man.

"And I'd like some courage," said the lion.

"And what about you?" the Wizard asked Dorothy. "What do you want?"

"I just want to go home to Kansas," said Dorothy.

"I will help you," said the Wizard. "But first, you must help me. Go and kill the last Wicked Witch in the land of Oz."

Dorothy and her friends were not very pleased. They didn't know how to kill the last Wicked Witch.

Dorothy, Toto, the scarecrow, the tin man and the lion went to find the Wicked Witch's castle.

Suddenly, the witch's flying monkeys came. They carried Dorothy, her friends and Toto back to the witch's castle.

33

The Wicked Witch wanted Dorothy's magic shoes.

"If I have the magic shoes, then I can be the wickedest witch the land of Oz has ever seen," she said.

But Dorothy wouldn't give her the magic shoes, so the witch made Dorothy work in her castle.

One day, the witch said, "If you don't give me your magic shoes, I will kill your little dog."

Dorothy was very angry. She took a bucket of water, and threw it all over the witch.

"You wicked girl, your water is killing me," said the Wicked Witch. And she disappeared.

So Dorothy and her friends went back to see the Wizard of Oz.

"Now we have helped you," said Dorothy, "please will you help us?"

So the Wizard of Oz gave the scarecrow some brains, the tin man a heart, and the lion some courage.

"Now I can think," said the scarecrow.

"Now I can love," said the tin man.

"And I will be a brave lion," said the lion.

"But what about Dorothy?"
said the scarecrow.

"I can't help her," said the
Wizard. "I don't know how to
send her home."

Suddenly, the Good Witch
appeared.

"Dorothy," said the Good Witch,
"you must ask your shoes to
take you home."

41

"Shoes, please take me home," said Dorothy. Suddenly she was back in her farmhouse with her aunt and uncle.

And Dorothy and Toto lived happily ever after.

Read It Yourself is a series of graded readers designed to give young children a confident and successful start to reading.

Level 4 is suitable for children who are ready to read longer stories with a wider vocabulary. The stories are told in a simple way and with a richness of language which makes reading a rewarding experience. Repetition of new vocabulary reinforces the words the child is learning and exciting illustrations bring the action to life.

About this book

At this stage children may prefer to read the story aloud to an adult without first discussing the pictures. Although children are now progressing towards silent, independent reading, they need to know that adult help and encouragement is readily available. When children meet a word they do not know, these words can be worked out by looking at the beginning letter (*what sound does this letter make?*) and other sounds the child recognises within the word. The child can then decide which word makes sense.

Nearly independent readers need lots of praise and encouragement.